S0-AVI-555

FIVE MINUTE
Nursery Tales

FIVE MINUTE
Nursery Tales

Written by
Derek Hall, Alison Morris
and Louisa Somerville

PARRAGON

Illustrated by
Jeremy Bays, Natalie Bould, Maureen Galvani, Mary Hall,
Virginia Margerison, Paula Martyr, Julia Oliver, Martin Orme,
Sara Silcock, Kerry Vaughan, Jenny Williams, Kirsty Wilson

Designed by Louise Millar

This edition is published
by Parragon 1999
PARRAGON
Queen Street House
4 Queen Street
Bath BA1 1HE, U.K.

Copyright © 1998 PARRAGON

Created and produced for Parragon by
Linda Watters Book Packaging
8 Trent Close, Shenley
Herts WD7 9HX, UK

All rights reserved. No part of this publication may be reproduced,
stored in a retrieval system, or transmitted in any form or by any
means, without the prior permission of the copyright holder.

ISBN 0-75253-314-2

Printed in Singapore

Contents

Mrs Mouse's Holiday

Mrs Mouse was very excited. All year she had been *so* busy. First there had been nuts and berries to gather in readiness for winter. Then she had needed to give her little house a big spring clean to make it nice and fresh. Now, as the warm sun shone down on the trees and flowers of her woodland home, she had promised herself a well-deserved holiday. But getting ready for holidays seemed to make one busier than ever! There was so much to do!

First she took out her little case, opened it and placed it carefully on her neatly made bed. Then she rushed to her cupboard and selected some fine holiday dresses. Back to her case she scuttled and laid them in. Now she chose several pairs of shoes – a nice pair of sandals for walking along the front in,

a pair of smart shoes for shopping in, an even smarter pair for going to dinner in, and another pair just in case!

"I'll need a couple of sun hats," she thought to herself, and so into the case they went as well. These were followed by a coat, some gloves and a scarf (just in case the breeze got up and it became cold). Then, in case it became very sunny, in went some sunglasses, some sun cream and a sunshade. But, oh dear, there were so many things in the case that it refused to shut. She tried sitting on it, and bouncing on it, but still it stubbornly would not close.

So out from the case came all the things that she had just put in, and Mrs Mouse scurried to the cupboard again and chose an even bigger case. This time they all fitted perfectly, and she shut the case with a big sigh of relief.

Now she was ready to go to the seaside for her holiday. She sat on the train, with her case on the rack above her head, munching her hazel nut sandwiches and looking eagerly out of the window hoping to see the sea. Finally, as the train chuffed around a bend, there it was! A great, deep blue sea shimmering in the sun, with white gulls soaring over the cliffs and headlands.

"I'm really looking forward to a nice, quiet rest," she said to herself.

Her guest house was very comfortable, and so close to the sea that she could smell the clean, salty air whenever she opened her window. "This is the life," she thought. "Nice and peaceful."

After she had put her clothes away, she put on her little swimming costume and her sun hat and packed her beach bag. Now she was ready for some peaceful sunbathing!

At the beach, she found herself a quiet spot, closed her eyes and was soon fast asleep. But not for long! A family of voles had arrived on the beach, and they weren't trying to have a quiet time at all. The youngsters in the family yelled at the top of their voices, splashed water everywhere, and sent their beach ball tumbling all over Mrs Mouse's neatly laid out beach towel.

Just as Mrs Mouse thought that it couldn't get any noisier, along came a crowd of ferrets. Now if you've ever sat on a beach next to a crowd of ferrets, you'll know what it's like. Their noisy shouting and singing made Mrs Mouse's head buzz.

Mrs Mouse couldn't stand it a moment longer. She was just wondering where she might find some peace and quiet when she spotted a rock just a little way out to sea.

"If I swim out to that rock," she thought, "I will surely have some peace and quiet there." So she gathered up her belongings and swam over to the rock. It was a bit lumpy, but at least it was quiet. Soon she was fast asleep again.

Just then the rock started to move slowly out to sea! It wasn't really a rock at all, you see, but a turtle which had been dozing near the surface. Off into the sunset it went, with Mrs Mouse dozing on its back, quite unaware of what was happening.

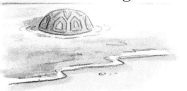

Eventually, the turtle came to a deserted island. At that moment, Mrs Mouse woke up. She looked at the empty beach, and without even knowing she had been sleeping on a turtle, she jumped off and swam to the shore, thinking it was the beach that she had just left.

Just then, the turtle swam off, and Mrs Mouse suddenly realised what had happened. For a moment she was horrified. But then she looked at the quiet, palm–fringed beach with no-one about but herself, and thought of the noisy beach she had just left.

"Well, perhaps this isn't such a bad place to spend a quiet holiday after all," she thought.

And that's just what she did. Day after day she lazed on her own private beach with no–one to disturb her. There were plenty of coconuts and fruits to eat, and she wanted for nothing. She even made herself a cozy bed from palm leaves.

Eventually, though, she started to miss her own little house in the woods and decided it was time to get back home. First she took half a coconut and nibbled out the tasty inside. "That will make a fine boat to sit in," she said.

Next she found a palm leaf and stuck it in the bottom of the shell. She took her little boat to the water's edge and, as the wind caught her palm leaf sail, off she floated back to the boarding house to get her belongings.

As she sailed back she thought, "This is the quietest holiday I've ever had. I may come back here next year!"

Morag the Witch

Morag was just an ordinary witch – until the day she enrolled for a course of advanced spell casting at the Wizard, Witch and Warlock Institute of Magic. For that was where she met Professor Fizzlestick. Now Professor Fizzlestick was a very wise old man indeed. Morag, on the other hand, was a very vain young witch who didn't know as much as she thought she did. She could turn people into frogs if they really deserved it, and do other simple spells like that, but she still had a lot to learn. The problem was, Morag thought she was the most perfect little witch in the whole wide world.

Morag's adventure started on her very first day at school. At the beginning of the day, after all the young witches and wizards had made friends and met the teachers, they were called in one by one to talk to Professor Fizzlestick.

"Now, young Morag Bendlebaum, I taught both your mother and your father," said the professor in a very serious voice, "and a very fine witch and wizard they turned out to be, too. So, what kind of witch do you think you are going to be?"

Without giving this any thought at all, Morag blurted out, "I'm better than my parents, and I'm probably better than you!"

This answer surprised even Morag, for although she thought this was true, she didn't actually mean to say it.

"Don't be surprised by your answers," said Professor Fizzlestick, "there is a truth spell in this room, and whatever you truly believe you must say. And I have to say that you appear to have an enormously high opinion of yourself. Why don't you tell me what makes you so very good?"

"I'm clever," said Morag, "and I'm good, and I'm always right."

"But what about your dark side?" said Professor Fizzlestick.

"I'm sorry to disappoint you," replied Morag quite seriously, "but I'm afraid I simply don't have a dark side."

13

"Well in that case I would like you to meet someone very close to you," said Professor Fizzlestick with a smile on his lips.

Morag looked over to where Professor Fizzlestick pointed, and was startled to see on the sofa next to her… herself!

As Morag stared open-mouthed with astonishment, the professor explained that if, as she believed, she was without a dark side, then there was absolutely nothing to worry about. "If, however," he continued, "you have deceived yourself, then I'm afraid you are in for a few surprises."

With that the professor dismissed them both from the room and told them to get to know each other. As Morag and her dark side stood outside the professor's room, Morag's dark side jumped and whooped for joy. "At last," she cried, "I'm free. I don't have to sit and listen to you telling me what's right all day; I don't have to keep persuading you to choose the biggest slice of cake before your brother – in fact, I don't, I repeat **don't,** have to do anything that you tell me at all."

So saying she broke into a run and rushed down the corridor, knocking over chairs and bumping into other little witches and wizards along the way. Morag was horrified. She would have to follow her dark side and stop her from causing trouble. Morag chased after her dark side and finally caught up with her at the chocolate machine. "Don't eat all that chocolate," cried Morag. "You know it's bad for your teeth and will ruin your appetite for lunch!"

"Tsk!" scoffed her dark side. "You might not want any chocolate but I certainly do!" And with that she ran off once more, dropping chocolate on to the freshly polished floor as well as pushing a big piece into her mouth.

Just then, the bell sounded for lunch. Although Morag felt she ought to find her dark side, she also knew that the bell was a command to go to the dining hall, and she mustn't disobey it. Morag sat down to lunch next to her friend, Topaz. She was just about to tell her what had happened, when she saw that Topaz was not eating her vegetables! Morag scolded Topaz for this, and gave her a lecture on eating healthily.

Topaz stared at Morag in amazement, then peered closely at her. "What's happened to you?" she asked.

Morag explained what had happened in Professor Fizzlestick's office, and then declared, "And you know, it's the best thing that has ever happened to me. I thought I was good before, but now I'm even better. I never want my dark side back again, but we must find her and lock her up so that she can do no harm."

Topaz agreed that they must find her dark side, but secretly hoped that she and Morag would be re-united. Morag wasn't Morag without her dark side.

After lunch, Morag went for her first lesson of the afternoon. When she walked into the classroom she discovered her dark side already there, busy preparing spells! Morag's dark side had already prepared a 'turning a nose into an elephant's trunk' spell and a 'turning skin into dragons' scales' spell and was just finishing off a 'turning your teacher into stone' spell!

Morag suddenly heard a trumpeting noise from the back of the classroom. She turned to find that the wizard twins, Denzil and Dorian Dillydally, had both sprouted huge grey trunks down to the ground where their noses had been. Morag rushed over to her dark side to make her change them back, but before she could reach her she tripped over a creature crouching down on the floor. It looked just like a dragon and it was wearing a purple and white spotted dress last seen on Betina Bumblebag. Morag's dark side was casting spells all over the place. "Oh, why doesn't the teacher stop her!" cried Morag to Topaz.

I'm sure you've guessed by now. Nice Miss Chuckle was entirely turned to stone from head to foot!

Just then Professor Fizzlestick walked into the classroom. Morag pointed to her dark side, still making spells at the front of the classroom.

16

"Lock her up immediately," Morag begged the professor.

"I'm afraid that you are the only one who can do that," said the wise old man. "The two of you are inseparable and you need each other. Without your dark side you would be unbearable and without you she is dreadful. Have I your permission to lock her back inside you?"

Even though Morag didn't want any part of her dark side back, she agreed reluctantly. Her dark side instantly disappeared, and Morag felt... wonderful! Oh, it was so good to be back to normal, to be basically good, but occasionally mischievous.

"Thank you," said Morag to the professor. "I think I've learned something very valuable today."

"There is good and bad in everyone," replied the professor, "even the most perfect of witches."

Morag blushed when she remembered what she had said earlier that morning, but she was so relieved to find she was normal that she really didn't mind. Morag and Topaz went back to the classroom to undo all the bad things Morag's dark side had done, but on the way they both felt a huge urge for a snack, so they stopped at the chocolate machine first!

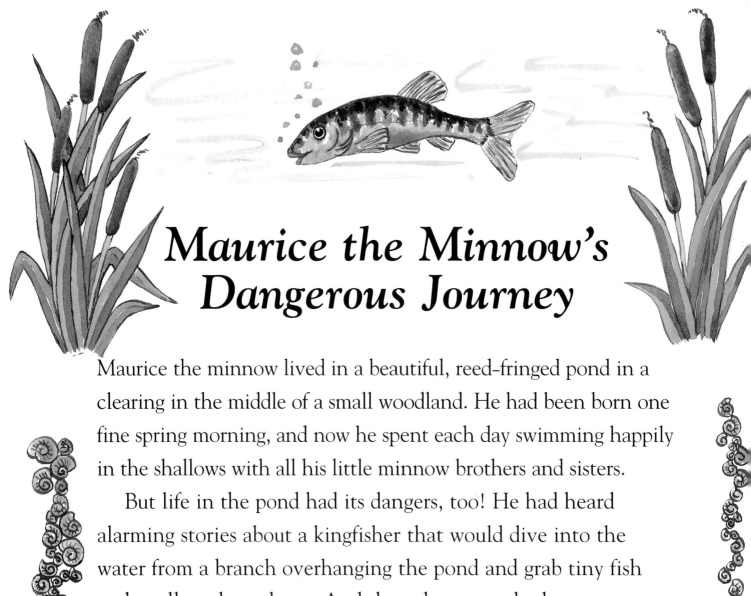

Maurice the Minnow's Dangerous Journey

Maurice the minnow lived in a beautiful, reed-fringed pond in a clearing in the middle of a small woodland. He had been born one fine spring morning, and now he spent each day swimming happily in the shallows with all his little minnow brothers and sisters.

But life in the pond had its dangers, too! He had heard alarming stories about a kingfisher that would dive into the water from a branch overhanging the pond and grab tiny fish and swallow them down. And then there was the heron – a great, grey, stalking bird that suddenly loomed into the shallows and snatched unsuspecting fish with its great beak.

But the stories Maurice feared most were the ones about Lucius the pike. Lucius had lived in the pond for longer than anyone could remember. Woe betide you if you met Lucius when he was hungry, for he would dart out from his hiding place among the water weeds, and you would be gone! Nothing ever escaped from his huge jaws, which were lined with needle-sharp teeth. Maurice had heard tales of Lucius swallowing fish bigger than Maurice could imagine – not to mention ducks, voles and other animals of the pond. Why, there was even a rumour that Lucius had once snatched a dog from the bank and taken it down to the depths of the pond to devour it!

Maurice's mother had said that the best way to avoid meeting Lucius was to always stay in the shallows, and never swim across the pond, for it was in the deep, dark waters that Lucius loved to hunt.

19

One sunny summer's day, Maurice and his brothers and sisters were swimming in the shallows as usual, when suddenly he felt himself being lifted up and out of the water. The next thing he knew he was flapping helplessly in the bottom of a net, gasping for breath. Mercifully, he soon found himself back in the water again, but it seemed different now. It was light all around and there were no welcoming, sheltering weeds to hide in. And where were all his brothers and sisters? Next, to his horror, he saw a huge, unfamiliar creature staring at him. He'd heard no stories about anything as big as this! The creature's head seemed so close that Maurice felt certain he was about to be eaten. But just as suddenly the creature seemed to move away, and Maurice felt himself being carried along in this new, strange, watery world.

Maurice was wondering if he was to be trapped in this new, small pond forever when just as suddenly as he seemed to have

entered the pond, he was now leaving it again. He felt himself falling down, down, until – with a splash – he was back in his own pond again. Or at least, it seemed like his pond, but nothing was quite as familiar as it had been. Finding a clump of water weed, he immediately dived under it for safety, while he considered what to do next.

"Hello, you're new here, aren't you?" a friendly voice said. Maurice looked round in surprise to find himself face to face with a frog. He told the frog about his horrible adventure while the frog listened patiently, nodding wisely from time to time.

"Well, we know what's happened to you, don't we?" said the frog when Maurice had finished. "You got caught in a little boy's fishing net. They're often about around here. I've no doubt the big creature you saw was just the little boy looking at you swimming in his jam jar full of water. And now he's decided to put you back. The only trouble is, you're far from home. You live on the other side of the pond. And to get you back means we have got to go on a very dangerous journey."

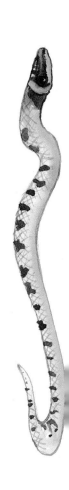

Maurice didn't like the sound of this at all, but he missed his family terribly and knew that he would never be able to get back home without the kind frog's help. So without more ado, the two of them set off for their journey across the deep, dark pond.

"Swim near the surface. It's safer," advised the frog, "but keep a close eye out for kingfishers."

They seemed to have been swimming for ages, when suddenly a great, dark shadow appeared beneath them.

"It's Lucius!" cried the frog in fright.

Before either of them could escape, they found themselves face to face with the dreaded pike. "Well, well," leered Lucius. "I can't believe my luck! A frog *and* a minnow. Lunch and supper together if I'm not mistaken!"

So saying, he opened his enormous jaws and was about to swallow them whole when – BOINK! – a huge, flat stone landed right on Lucius's head. Dazed, Lucius sank slowly towards the bottom of the pond.

"Quick! It's our chance to escape!" yelled the frog. The two friends swam for their lives. Maurice kept thinking that any moment Lucius would reappear, but he needn't have worried. Lucius had too big a headache to think about hunting for a while yet!

Then suddenly Maurice was home. He recognised his own little part of the pond, and there swimming in the shallows was his family.

"I can't thank you enough," said Maurice gratefully to the frog. "But what *did* happen to Lucius?"

"You can thank the little boy who caught you in the net for our escape," said the frog. "He was skimming stones across the pond and luckily Lucius's head got in the way!"

Maurice decided that he'd had quite enough adventures for one day, and found himself a cosy piece of water weed to hide under. Soon he was fast asleep.

The Magic Tree

Tommy rubbed his eyes, blinked hard, and looked out of his bedroom window again. But it was still there – an enormous oak tree that definitely hadn't been there yesterday! If it had been there, he'd have known all about it for sure. For a start he would have climbed up it, for Tommy loved nothing better than climbing trees.

No, this tree was definitely not there yesterday! Tommy sat staring at the tree in wonder and disbelief. The tree stood there, outside his bedroom window, with its huge, spreading branches almost asking to be climbed. Tommy wondered how on earth it had suddenly got there, but he decided that before he wondered about that too much, he had better go and climb it first. After all, there was always time later to wonder about things but never enough time to do things, he thought.

As soon as he was dressed, he ran outside to take a closer look at the new tree. It seemed just like any other big oak tree. It had lots of wide, inviting branches and lots of green, rounded leaves. And it had deep, furrowed bark just like any other oak tree.

Tommy couldn't resist any longer. On to the lowest branch he stepped and then up to the next. The tree seemed so easy to climb. There were branches everywhere. In no time at all, he was in a green, leafy canopy. He couldn't even see the ground any more. But something seemed not quite right. The branches beneath his feet seemed to be so big now that he could stand up on them and walk in any direction. And the branches all around him seemed just like trees themselves. In fact, he suddenly realised that he wasn't any longer climbing a tree, but standing in a whole forest full of trees.

Tommy didn't like this at all, and thought he had better get down. But where was down? All he could see were tall, swaying trees and here and there a twisty path leading off even deeper into the forest. Tommy didn't know how he had done it, but he had somehow got himself completely lost in a forest, and he hadn't even had breakfast yet!

Worse still, it seemed to be getting dark. "Quick, over here!" a voice suddenly called out. Tommy was very startled, but he was even more startled when he saw that the voice belonged to a squirrel.

"You can speak!" blurted out Tommy.

"Of course I can speak!" snapped the squirrel. "Now listen. You are in great danger, and there's no time to lose if we are to save you from the clutches of the evil Wizard of the Woods."

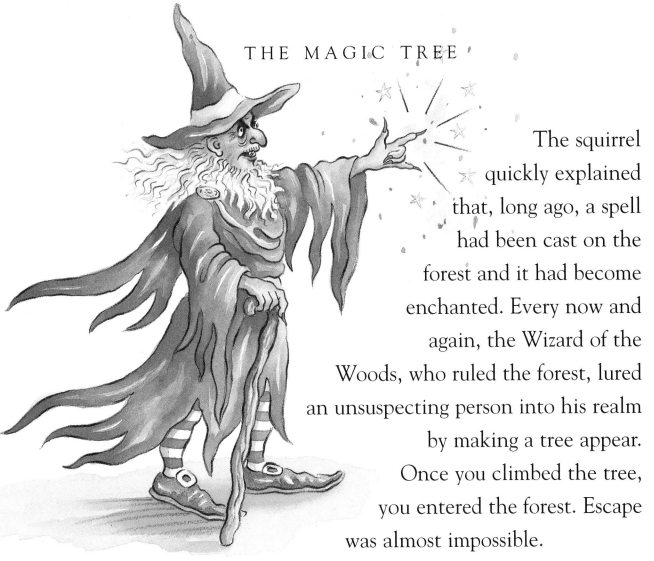

The squirrel quickly explained that, long ago, a spell had been cast on the forest and it had become enchanted. Every now and again, the Wizard of the Woods, who ruled the forest, lured an unsuspecting person into his realm by making a tree appear. Once you climbed the tree, you entered the forest. Escape was almost impossible.

"But why does the Wizard of the Woods want to lure people into the forest?" asked Tommy, rather hoping that he didn't have to hear the answer.

"To turn them into fertilizer to make the trees grow," said the squirrel.

Tommy didn't really know what fertilizer was, but it sounded rather nasty. He was pleased when the squirrel suddenly said, "There is just one way to get you out of here. But we must hurry. Soon it will be dark and the Wizard of the Woods will awake. Once he awakes, he will smell your blood and he will capture you."

With that, the squirrel jumped up the nearest tree. "Follow me," he said.

Tommy immediately climbed after the squirrel. "Where are we going?" he panted as they climbed higher and higher.

"To the top of the tallest tree in the forest," the squirrel answered as they clambered from tree to tree, climbing ever higher.

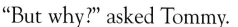

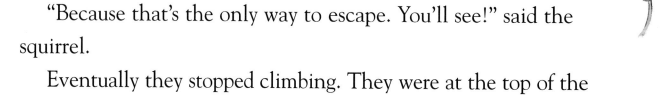

"But why?" asked Tommy.

"Because that's the only way to escape. You'll see!" said the squirrel.

Eventually they stopped climbing. They were at the top of the tallest tree in the forest. Below them and around them was nothing but more trees. Tommy looked up, and at last he could see the clear, twilight sky. He also noticed something rather strange. All the leaves at the top of the tallest tree were enormous.

"Quick, time is running out," said the squirrel. "Sit on this leaf and hold tight."

Tommy sat on one of the huge leaves. The squirrel whistled, and before Tommy could blink he had been joined by a hundred more squirrels. They each took hold of the branch to which the leaf was attached. With a great heave, they pulled and pulled until the branch was bent backwards. Suddenly they let go. With a mighty "TWANG", the branch, with Tommy and the leaf attached, sprang forward. As it did so Tommy and the leaf were launched into the air. High above the trees they soared until, ever so slowly, they began to float down to earth. Down, down, they went, until they landed with a bump.

Tommy opened his eyes to find himself on his bedroom floor. He ran over to the window and looked out. The magic tree was nowhere to be seen. It had gone as quickly as it had appeared. But perhaps it had never been there at all. Maybe it was just a dream. What do you think?

Catswhiskers

Catswhiskers was a pyjama case cat, and a very fine-looking pyjama case cat at that. Susie's granny had sewn him together when Susie was only four years old. It had taken Susie's granny quite a long time to make Catswhiskers. Every night she had sat by the fire carefully cutting and sewing, until he was perfect. Catswhiskers' body was made from the finest black velvet. He had beautiful red glass eyes, a bushy tail and the longest whiskers you have ever seen. That is how he got the name Catswhiskers. Catswhiskers sat on the end of Susie's bed, looking at all the toys in the bedroom in that slightly snooty way that cats have of looking at things.

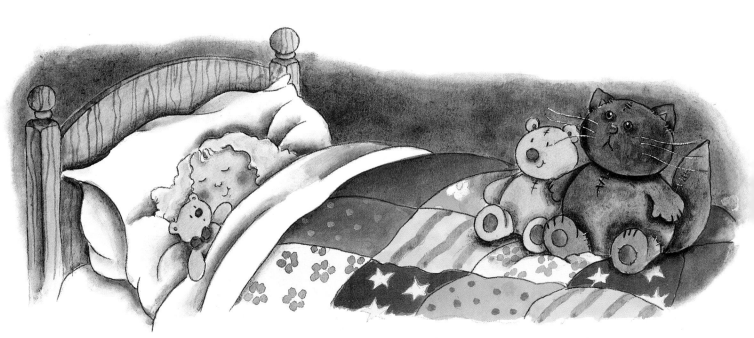

When Susie was asleep, or playing in another room, Catswhiskers and all the toys would talk to each other. But Catswhiskers was bored with talking to the toys. Jenny the ragdoll was – well – just a ragdoll. "What could a ragdoll possibly have to say that would be of interest to a velvet pyjama case cat?" thought Catswhiskers.

Then there was Neddy the rocking horse. He was a perfectly pleasant rocking horse as far as rocking horses went, but he only ever seemed to want to talk about how nice and shiny he was, and how he thought he was Susie's favourite toy. Even the alphabet bricks, the jack-in-the-box and the brightly coloured ball seemed to have nothing to say of interest to Catswhiskers. He sighed and looked at the window, wondering if life was more exciting outside.

31

One day, he decided he'd had enough of life in the bedroom with all the toys, and that he would venture outside to see if he could meet someone more interesting to talk to. So that night, when it was dark and Susie was asleep, he crept carefully to the open bedroom window and jumped out. It was a clear, cold, moonlit night. Catswhiskers shivered a little to find it so cold outside, and he maybe shivered a little more because he was also rather frightened. But he was very excited to be in the outside world, too, and he soon forgot about the cold and his fear.

He walked along the fence to the end of Susie's garden and jumped down into the garden next door. He had no sooner landed when he heard a fierce growl and saw two big, black eyes glinting in the moonlight.

It was Barker, next door's dog – and he didn't like cats at all. With a loud bark, Barker came rushing towards Catswhiskers. His mouth was open wide and Catswhiskers could see his big, sharp teeth. In fact, he thought that he could see all the way down into Barker's stomach! Catswhiskers only just had time to leap back on to the fence as Barker, jaws still snapping, gave chase.

"Phew, what a narrow escape," gasped Catswhiskers. "I didn't realise dogs were so unfriendly!"

He was wondering where it might be safe to go next when he heard a low, hissing voice behind him. "Hey, velvet cat," hissed the voice. "What do you think you are doing on *our* patch?"

Catswhiskers turned round to see the biggest, meanest-looking cat he had ever set eyes on. And behind *him* were several more mean-looking cats, all coming slowly towards Catswhiskers with their sharp claws at the ready. Catswhiskers didn't wait a second longer. He simply ran for his life.

Now he was very frightened. He was also feeling cold and hungry. He wished that he was still in the warm safety of Susie's bedroom with the other toys. Just as he was thinking that the outside world was perhaps a bit *too* exciting, he heard the sound of a van approaching. It suddenly stopped, its glaring headlights shining straight at him. On the side of the van were the words STRAY CAT CATCHER.

Out of the van stepped a man carrying a big net. Catswhiskers thought he knew just who that net was for, and decided that it was definitely time to go!

Without thinking about the dangers he might find himself in if he came face to face again with gangs of sharp-clawed cats or fierce, barking dogs, he ran back towards Susie's house as fast as his velvet legs could carry him. At last he reached the window and jumped thankfully back inside.

Snuggled down again on the warm bed with all his familiar friends around him, Catswhiskers decided that perhaps this was the best life for a pyjama case cat after all.

The Princess and the Snowman

One morning Princess Bella looked out of her bedroom window and saw that the palace was covered in a thick layer of snow. Snow lay on the turrets and along the tops of the walls. There was snow in the well and snow on the guards' hats. The palace garden was so deep with snow it looked as though it was covered in delicious icing. The snow looked fresh, inviting and untouched – apart from a line of paw prints made by Bella's pet cat, Beau.

The princess clapped her hands with glee. "I'm going to make a snowman," she cried, and rushed off to find her warmest coat and gloves. Soon she was busy in the garden rolling a great ball of snow for the snowman's body and another one for his head.

At last the snowman was finished, and she put an old hat on his head and a scarf around his neck.

"Now," thought Princess Bella, "he needs a face." Turning to Beau she said, "Go and find the snowman a nose."

"Meiow!" said Beau and trotted off. Bella found three lumps of coal and stuck them in a row on the snowman's head to make a mouth. Then she stuck a stone on each side of his head for ears. Beau came back with a piece of carrot in her mouth.

"Well done, Beau," said Bella. "That's perfect for a nose." And she stuck the carrot in place.

At that moment there was a call from a palace window. "Bella, Bella! Come inside at once. It's time for your lessons," called the queen. Bella ran indoors and, do you know, she forgot all about giving the snowman a pair of eyes.

"I wonder when the princess will come and give me my eyes," thought the snowman wistfully. "I'd better keep my wits about me." He listened hard with his stone ears and sniffed with his carrot nose, but there was no-one there.

Night came and all the lights in the palace went out. In the middle of the night, a storm blew up. The windows of the palace rattled, the trees creaked and groaned and the wind moaned. The snowman strained his stone ears even harder and now he could hear a fearsome icy jangle and a piercing, shrieking laugh. It was the Ice Queen. As she blew past the snowman, he felt the Ice Queen's cold breath on his snowy cheek and the touch of her icicle fingers on his snowy brow. The snowman shivered with fear. Now he heard the Ice Queen's icy tap, tap, tap on the palace door and her howl as she slipped through the keyhole. There was silence for a while, then suddenly the snowman heard a window being flung open and the Ice Queen's cruel laugh.

"She's leaving," thought the snowman with relief.

But what was this? Now he could hear the sound of a girl sobbing and as the Ice Queen passed he heard

Princess Bella's voice calling, "Help me!" Then there was silence again, save for the sound of the wind in the trees.

"She's carried off the princess," thought the snowman. "There's only one thing to do!" He drew his breath and with all his might he shouted through his coal lips, "Heeelp!" He thought to himself, "No-one will hear my shouts above the noise of the wind."

But soon he felt a warm glow on his cheek. "Can I help?" said a soft, kindly voice. "I am the South Wind and I can see you're in trouble."

The snowman could hardly believe his stone ears. "Oh, yes, please help," he cried. "The Ice Queen has carried off Princess Bella and I'm afraid she may die of cold."

"I'll see what I can do," said the South Wind gently, and she started to blow a warm wind. She blew and she blew and soon the Ice Queen's icy arms began to melt. Then Bella was able to slip from her cold grasp.

"It was the snowman who saved you," whispered the South Wind in Bella's ear as she carried her back to the palace.

Bella could hear the drip, drip, sound of snow being melted by the South Wind's warm breath. As she reached the palace gate, the sun was rising and the snow in the garden was turning to slush. "I must see my snowman before he is gone," she thought.

There he was on the lawn. His hat was starting to slide off his head and his mouth was all crooked. She rushed over to him and to her astonishment he spoke.

"Please give me my eyes before I melt completely," he begged.

"Yes, of course I will," Bella replied. Quickly she fixed two pieces of coal in place on his melting face.

"You are so lovely," said the snowman, looking at her with his coal eyes. "I have one last request before I'm gone. Will you marry me?"

"Why, I will!" said Bella without thinking twice – for how could she refuse the request of the one who had saved her from the Ice Queen?

Bella could not bear to think that the snowman was melting away. She glanced down so that he would not see that she was crying.

"Bella," he said. She looked up and there standing before her was a prince. For once in her life she was speechless.

"Long ago, the Ice Queen carried me away – just like she did to you. She cast a spell on me that meant I could only return to earth as falling snow. But by agreeing to marry me you have broken the spell," said the prince.

And so Bella and the prince were married, and lived happily ever after.

The Singing Bear

Long ago, there lived a young boy named Peter. He was a gentle lad who loved all creatures, but most of all he loved the animals and birds of the forest. Many a time he had mended a jay's broken wing, or set a badger free from a cruel trap.

One day, the fair came to town and Peter was very excited. He could see brightly coloured tents being put up in the field and carts arriving with mysterious looking loads. As soon as the fair was open Peter was off with his penny in his pocket to try his luck. First of all he had a go at the coconut shy. Then he tried to climb the greasy pole. Finally, he used his last farthing on the tombola stall. He was about to head for home when out of the corner of his eye he caught a glimpse of a dreadful sight. Lying in a cage, looking sad and forlorn, was a large brown bear. On a small plate at the front of the cage was the bear's name: Lombard. He looked so dejected that Peter immediately vowed to set him free. The cage was strongly padlocked and Peter knew not how he could break the lock. He turned to make his way home, with the bear gazing pitifully after him.

That night, Peter tossed and turned in his bed. What was he to do? He wasn't strong enough to break into the bear's cage and his keeper would surely not agree to set him free. In the middle of the night, he resolved to return to the fairground to comfort the bear.

He slipped out of bed and made his way by the light of the moon back to the fairground. To his astonishment he found the bear singing a song to himself in a beautiful voice. For a while Peter listened to the lovely sound of the bear's singing. Then he had an idea. He remembered a piece of paper he had seen pinned to the palace gate.

Lombard

"Don't cry, Lombard," he said. "I think I know a way to get you out of here. But first you must teach me your song." The bear was happy to oblige and soon the two of them were singing the song together. Then Peter said, "I must go, but I'll be back tomorrow. And remember, when you see me, be ready to sing your song."

The next day, Peter put on his very best clothes and set off for the palace. Pinned to the gate was the piece of paper, just as Peter had remembered. On the paper was written in a handsome script: *The King Requires a Minstrel with a Fine Voice. Apply Within.*

Peter knocked at the gate. He was shown into a beautiful golden gallery where a row of minstrels were waiting to be auditioned. A courtier rang a little bell for silence, and in came the king. He sat down at his great gold throne.

"Let the audition begin," cried the king. The first minstrel stepped forward. He sang a song in a sweet, high voice that tugged at the heart and reduced the court to tears. The next minstrel sang in a deep, rich voice that sent shivers down the spine, so that the birds in the trees stopped singing to listen. The next minstrel sang a song that was so witty and amusing that the entire court wept with laughter.

At last it was Peter's turn. He stepped forward, gave a deep bow and said, "I beg your majesty's permission to perform my song out of doors, so that all the wild creatures of the forest might hear it, too."

"What a strange request!" said the king. However, if the truth be told, he had grown quite sleepy listening to so many beautiful songs and thought the fresh air might liven him up. "Very well, but it had better be worth it!" he said, giving Peter a fierce look.

"Follow me!" called Peter. He led the king, the court and all the minstrels out of the palace gates and down the road.

"Where are we going?" and "This is very untoward," they muttered. At last they reached the fairground, but Peter didn't stop until he was in view of Lombard's cage. Lombard saw him and Peter winked at the bear.

"This is where I'd like to sing for you," said Peter to the king.

The king's royal eyebrows rose higher and higher as he looked around him. "Well, I must say this is very odd indeed! However, as we've come this far, we may as well hear your song. Proceed!" said the king.

Peter opened his mouth and mimed the words while Lombard sang. It was the most beautiful song that anyone had ever heard. By the end of the song, the king was sobbing tears of joy, mirth and sorrow all together.

"That was the finest song I ever heard," he said. "You have won the audition and I would like you to be my minstrel."

Peter took another low bow. "Sire," he said. "Would that I could accept, but in all honesty it was not I who sang but my friend, Lombard the bear." Everyone gasped as they saw the bear in his cage.

For a moment the king looked furious. But then he began to smile and said, "I praise you for your honesty, Peter, and I would very much like to have Lombard for my minstrel. Chancellor, bring me the royal purse."

The king paid Lombard's keeper handsomely, who was then delighted to set the bear free. Lombard became the king's minstrel and was famous throughout the land, and from then on Peter went to the palace each day and sang duets with his friend, the bear. And it is said that, in the end, Peter married the king's daughter.

The King Who Ate Too Much

Long ago, in a kingdom far, far away, there lived a greedy king.
Now the thing that this king loved, more than anything else in
the whole world, was food. He simply couldn't get enough of it.
Ever since he was a little prince, he had been allowed to eat
whatever he wanted, whenever he wanted it. And because he
was always eating, he just got fatter and fatter and fatter with
every day that passed.

When he became king, his appetite seemed to get even
bigger! As soon as he woke in the morning, he would have his
servants bring him an enormous breakfast. After eating several
huge, steaming bowls of porridge, he would eat slice after slice of
hot, buttered toast and jam, followed by all the boiled eggs that
the royal chickens could lay.

In case he got a little hungry mid-morning, he would have a snack – usually ten or more chocolate cakes, washed down with as many cups of tea!

At lunchtime, the table would groan with the weight of all the pies, sandwiches, fruit and biscuits that the greedy king was about to gobble down.

For afternoon tea, it would be cakes, cakes and more cakes.

But the king's biggest meal was supper! The royal cooks toiled for most of the day to prepare this feast. When it was time for the king to eat, one servant after another would carry in great bowls of steaming soup, plates of fish of every kind, followed by huge roasts and dishes of vegetables. Down it all went, followed by fruit and jelly. At last, the king would be full and he would retire to his bed for the night.

But the king's greedy eating habits also made him a very thoughtless king. No-one dared tell him that much of the wealth of the kingdom had to be spent on his huge meals. In the meantime, his loyal subjects were going hungry and becoming poor and needy.

One day, just after the king had eaten his usual big lunch, he began to feel very strange. Not only did he feel even bigger than usual, he also began to feel very light. Suddenly, without any warning, he started floating up from the table and into the air like a big balloon.

"Help! Get me down!" he cried.

50

The royal courtiers and servants jumped up and down and tried in vain to grab the king as he floated upwards, but in no time at all he had floated out of reach. Before anyone knew it, he had floated out of the castle window. Out across the royal grounds he went, over the river and towards the woods and mountains of his kingdom.

"Wooaa-aaah!" cried the king, as he disappeared from view.

Soon, the king began to float over a small farm. He looked down and saw the farmer's children, dressed only in rags, searching for firewood. Some thin, hungry cows stood nearby chewing on a few meagre pieces of hay.

Over the next farm he floated, and a similar sad scene met his gaze. Dressed in rags, a poor farmer and his family toiled their soil hoping to grow enough to eat.

Next he floated over a small village. Everywhere he looked he saw shabby, run-down houses in need of repair and people in the streets begging for money.

Every farm and every village the king floated over told the same story of hunger and misery. The king suddenly felt very sad and very ashamed. He had been so busy enjoying himself eating that he hadn't given a thought to the plight of his subjects. While he was getting fatter and fatter, they were all getting thinner and poorer.

Now, a gust of wind was blowing the king back towards his castle. As he was passing over the castle, he suddenly felt himself falling. Down, down, he went until he landed back into the castle grounds with a great thud and a bounce.

That very day, the king sent out a royal proclamation. All his loyal subjects were to come to the castle for a huge feast, after which they would all be given a purse full of gold.

As for the king, he was never greedy again. Instead of spending all his money on food for himself, he gave enough to all the people in the land so that they would never be hungry or poor again.

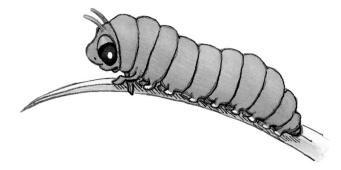

The Jealous Caterpillar

One spring day a green caterpillar sat on a leaf. He watched a beautiful butterfly flutter past him on the breeze. "It's not fair. Here I am stuck on this boring leaf with nothing to do and nowhere to go while that lucky creature can fly across the world and see far-off lands," thought the caterpillar crossly. "And what's more," he continued to himself, "not only has that butterfly got wings with which to fly, but he's beautiful, too. Look at poor me. I'm just a dull green. No-one will notice me because I'm the same colour as the leaf." The caterpillar really did feel very sorry for himself, and rather jealous. "Go and enjoy yourself. Don't worry about me," he called spitefully to the butterfly.

But the butterfly hadn't heard a single word the caterpillar had been muttering, and soon he flew away. The caterpillar suddenly decided that he was going to be like the butterfly. "I'll learn how to fly and I'll paint myself lovely colours so that I look beautiful, too," he thought. He looked around for something to paint himself with but, of course, there was nothing at all on the leaf. Then he tried to fly. He launched himself from his leaf and tried to flap his tail, but all he did was land on the leaf below.

Along came a ladybird. "Aha!" thought the caterpillar. "Here's a beautiful creature who knows how to fly. I'll ask her to teach me." So the caterpillar said, "Hello, I've been admiring your beautiful wingcase. Could you tell me how I, too, could be beautiful? And can you teach me to fly?"

The ladybird looked at the caterpillar. "Be patient and wait a while," she said wisely, "and soon enough you'll get what you want." And with that the ladybird went on her way.

"Whatever can she mean? She's just too proud to teach me," the caterpillar thought jealously.

Some time later a bee buzzed past and landed on a nearby leaf. "Aha!" thought the caterpillar. "Here's a beautiful creature who knows how to fly. I'll ask him to teach me." So the caterpillar said, "Hello, I've been admiring your beautiful striped back. Could you tell me how I, too, could be beautiful? And can you teach me to fly?"

The bee looked at the caterpillar. "You'll find out soon enough, young man," said the bee sternly. And with that he went on his way.

"Whatever can he mean? He's just too haughty to teach me," the caterpillar thought jealously.

Now a while later along came a bird. "Aha!" thought the caterpillar once more. "Here's a beautiful creature who knows how to fly. I'll ask him to teach me." So once again the caterpillar said, "Hello, I've been admiring your beautiful feathers. Could you tell me how I, too, could be beautiful? And can you teach me to fly?"

The bird looked at the caterpillar and thought to himself slyly that here was a very silly caterpillar, but he would make a tasty snack for his chicks. "Let's see if I can trick him," he thought.

"I can't give you wings and I can't make you beautiful. But I can show you the world. I expect you'd like to see the world, wouldn't you, little caterpillar?" said the bird.

"Oh, yes!" said the caterpillar in great excitement.

"Climb upon my back then, little caterpillar!" said the crafty bird.

The caterpillar did as he was told and the bird flew off towards his nest. At first the caterpillar clung tightly to the bird's back but soon he felt quite sleepy and eventually he dozed off and slipped from the bird's back. Down he fell through the air and landed on a leaf, but still he didn't wake up. Soon he was wrapped in a soft, brown, papery cocoon from which he would not wake up for a long while.

Meanwhile, the bird reached his nest. "Look at the treat I've brought you," he said to his chicks.

They looked very puzzled. "What treat, Dad?" one of them piped up.

"This nice juicy caterpillar," said the bird, shaking the feathers on his back. "Climb down, little caterpillar," he said. But of course there was nothing there. Now it was the father's turn to look puzzled, while the chicks laughed at him.

"Well, I must have dropped him," he said. "I've never done that before," he added. He flew out of the nest in search of the caterpillar but he was nowhere to be seen. Once he saw a strange brown, papery parcel on a leaf, but in the end the bird had to return to the nest with his beak empty.

A long while later the caterpillar woke up. "I must get out of this stuffy wrapping," he thought, as he pushed his way out. He stood on the leaf and yawned and stretched. As he stretched, he noticed to his amazement two pairs of beautiful wings spreading out on either side of his body. "Are they really mine?" he wondered. He tried lifting and turning them and yes, he could make them work. He looked at his reflection in a raindrop and saw a lovely butterfly staring back at him. "So the ladybird and the bee were right," he exclaimed. "How foolish I was to be a jealous caterpillar," he declared to a passing ant, "for now I am a beautiful butterfly after all."

Ursula's Umbrella

Ursula was a little girl who longed for adventure. She loved reading stories about far-away places and explorers, and even children like herself who had amazing adventures. "Why doesn't anything interesting ever happen to me?" she sighed. "How I wish I could fly to the moon or dive to the deepest part of the ocean. What fun it would be!"

One windy day, Ursula went out for a walk. She took her umbrella with her because it looked as though it might be going to rain. Ursula's umbrella was red with a shiny black handle. It was also very large indeed. People used to laugh as Ursula walked along the street with her umbrella up. It looked so big and Ursula was so small that it seemed as though the umbrella was walking along all by itself!

As Ursula walked up the street she felt a few raindrops on her nose. "Better put up my umbrella," she thought. She unfurled her umbrella and lifted it up above her head. As she did so, a great gust of wind came and swept her right off the pavement. It carried her past the upstairs windows of the houses, past the roofs and the chimney pots and up, up, into the sky. Ursula clung tightly to the umbrella handle. She was surprised to find she didn't feel the least bit frightened. No, not a bit. She felt very excited. She looked down and saw streets and factories whizzing past far below. Then she saw fields and something that looked like a silver thread snaking through the countryside. "A river!" thought Ursula.

Now she could see the coastline, and soon the umbrella was carrying her out over the ocean. At first when she looked down the sea was grey, but gradually it turned to the deepest blue with frothy white waves. "How I'd love a swim," thought Ursula. At that moment she felt the umbrella starting to descend. Looking down she could see that they were heading for an island in the middle of the ocean. Soon she was floating past the tops of palm trees and, as she touched the ground, she felt sand under her feet.

"I'm going for a swim!" said Ursula to herself. She folded up her umbrella and set off to the beach. The water felt deliciously warm as Ursula paddled about. She looked down and saw that the water was amazingly clear. She could see brightly coloured fish darting in and out of the coral. "Wow!" exclaimed Ursula out loud and then "Wow!" again, though this time much louder as she looked up and saw a black fin skimming through the water towards her. "Shark!" she shrieked, but no-one heard.

Then all of a sudden a gust of wind made her umbrella unfurl itself and float towards her in the water, like a boat. Ursula made a dash for the umbrella, hurled herself into it and floated away across the sea. "That was quite an adventure!" she thought.

After a while, Ursula looked out over the rim of the umbrella and saw that it was heading for the shore again. This time, when Ursula stepped out of the umbrella, she found that she was at the edge of a jungle. Folding up the umbrella, she set off into the forest. She followed an overgrown path through the trees. "I wonder where this leads?" thought Ursula. She wiped her brow and swatted the insects that flew in front of her face. Deeper and deeper into the jungle she went.

Suddenly she heard the sound of rushing water and found herself standing on the banks of a river. All at once she heard another sound. It was the crashing noise of some enormous beast approaching through the trees.

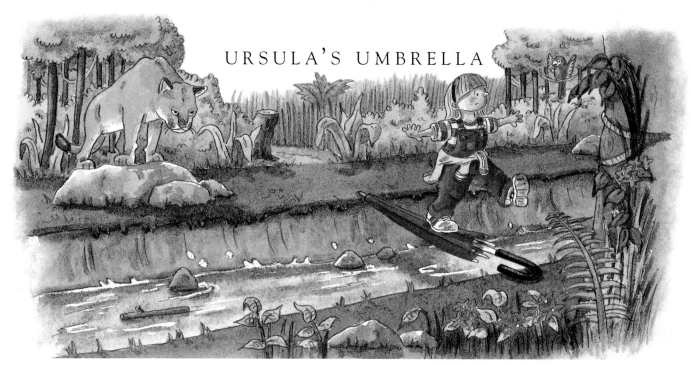

Where could she run to? Suddenly she felt the umbrella being blown from her hand. To her amazement it fell to the ground, stretching right across the river like a bridge. Ursula walked over to the other side, not daring to look down at the torrent below. When she was safely on the far bank she looked back to see a large puma, with glittering green eyes, glaring at her from the opposite bank. "That was a lucky escape!" thought Ursula.

Ursula could see a mountain through the trees and decided to head towards it. "I'll be able to get a good view from the top and maybe find my way home," she thought. She struggled on through the forest and eventually found herself at the foot of the mountain. There seemed to be no way up the sheer rock face.

Ursula was on the point of despair when suddenly another great gust of wind blew up. It carried Ursula, clinging to her opened umbrella, all the way up to the top of the mountain.

64

URSULA'S UMBRELLA

At the top of the mountain, the umbrella let her gently down again and her feet landed in deep snow. By now it was blowing a blizzard and she could not see anything except white snowflakes in all directions. "There's only one thing to do," thought Ursula. She put the umbrella on the snow, sat on it and whizzed all the way down the other side of the mountain.

When she reached the bottom, to her surprise, the umbrella sledge didn't stop but carried on through the snowstorm until eventually, after a very long time, it came to a halt right outside her own front door. "Well, that was quite an adventure," said Ursula, shaking the snow off the umbrella, before folding it up.

She stepped inside the front door. "Wherever have you been?" said her mother. "You look as though you've been to the ends of the Earth and back."

"Well I have," Ursula was about to say. But then she thought that no-one would believe her and it was nicer to keep her adventures to herself. And that is what she did.

The Greedy Hamster

There was once a hamster named Harry. He was a very greedy hamster. As soon as his food was put in his cage he gobbled it all up, and then he would push his little nose through the bars in the hope that something else to eat might come within reach. From his cage he could see all manner of delicious food on the kitchen table – and the smells! The scent of freshly baked bread was enough to send him spinning round in his exercise wheel with frustration.

"It's not fair!" he grumbled to himself. "They're all eating themselves silly out there and here am I simply starving to death!" (At this point he would usually remember the large meal he had just eaten and that his tummy was indeed still rather full.)

"If only I could get out of this beastly cage, I could feast on all the food I deserve," he announced to himself, and the thought of all those tasty morsels made his mouth water.

One night after the family had gone to bed, Harry was having one last spin in his wheel before retiring to his sawdust mattress. As he spun around, he heard an unfamiliar squeaky noise.

"That's funny," thought Harry. "The little girl oiled my wheel only today. It surely can't need oiling again." He stopped running and got off the wheel, but the squeak continued. Harry sat quite still on his haunches and listened intently. Then he realised it was the door to his cage squeaking. The door! The door was flapping open. The little girl had not closed it properly before she went to bed. Harry did a little dance of glee. Then he went to the door and looked cautiously out in case there was any danger. But all seemed to be well. The cat was asleep on a chair. The dog was sleeping soundly on the floor.

Now, as well as being a greedy hamster, Harry was also clever. Once outside the cage, the first thing he did was look at the catch to see how it worked. Yes! He was pretty sure he could work out how to open it from the inside now. Harry sniffed the air. There were some tasty titbits left over from a birthday party on the table. He could smell the sugar icing, and soon he was on the table, cramming his mouth with odds and ends of cheese sandwiches and pieces of chocolate cake. When he had eaten his fill, he stuffed his cheek pouches with ginger biscuits and ran back into his cage, closing the door behind him.

"Good!" thought Harry. "Now I will never be hungry again."

The next night Harry let himself out of his cage and helped himself to food, and again the next night and the night after that. He feasted on everything and anything – nuts, bananas, pieces of bread, left-over jelly and slices of pizza were all pushed into his greedy mouth. Each time he returned to his cage he filled his cheeks with more and more food. He did not notice that he was getting fatter and fatter, although he was aware that he could no longer run round in his wheel without falling off! Then one night, he undid the door catch but found he was simply too wide to get through the door!

For a while Harry sat in a very bad temper in the corner of the cage. His cheeks were still bulging with food from his last midnight feast, but the greedy hamster wanted more. Then he had an idea. "I'll get that lazy cat to help," he thought. He squealed at the top of his voice until the cat, who had been dreaming of rats, woke up with a start.

"What do you want?" she hissed at Harry. Harry explained his problem.

"Of course, I'd be only too pleased to help," said the crafty cat, thinking to herself here was an extra dinner! With her strong claws she bent back the door frame of the cage, until there was just enough room for Harry to squeeze through. Then, with a mighty swipe of her paw, she caught him and gobbled him whole. She felt extremely full, what with Harry and all his food inside her. She could barely crawl back to her chair and soon she was fast asleep again and snoring loudly with her mouth open. Inside her tummy Harry, too, felt very uncomfortable. Every time the cat snored, it sounded like a thunderstorm raging around his head.

"I must get out of here," he thought, and headed for the cat's open jaws. But he was far too fat to get out again. Then he had another idea. Through the cat's jaws he could see the dog lying on the floor.

"Help! Help!" he squeaked. The dog woke up to a very strange sight. There was the cat lying on the chair snoring, but she also seemed to be squeaking, "Help!" The dog put his head on one side. He was very perplexed. Then he saw a pair of beady eyes and some fine whiskers inside the cat's mouth. It was Harry!

"Get me out of here, please," pleaded Harry.

Now the dog did not very much like the cat, so he was quite willing to help the hamster.

"I'll stick my tail in the cat's mouth. Then you hang on while I pull you out," said the dog. "But mind you don't make a sound and wake the cat, or she'll surely bite my tail!" The dog gingerly put the tip of his tail inside the cat's open jaws, just far enough for Harry's little paws to grab hold. Then he pulled with all his might. Out popped Harry and out of Harry popped all the food he'd stored in his cheeks – peanuts, an apple core and a slice of jam tart!

"Thank you, thank you," gasped Harry as he made a dash for his cage and slammed the door shut. "I think I'll stay in my cage from now on and just stick to the food I'm given!"

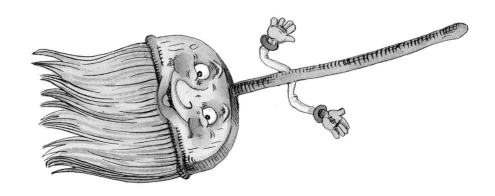

The Naughty Broom

"Goodness me, what a lot of dirt and dust there is all over this kitchen floor," said the maid. She was a very house-proud maid, and didn't like dirt and dust on her floor one little bit. Out came the broom from its place in the cupboard in the corner, and soon the maid was busily sweeping the floor and brushing all the dirt and dust into a big dustpan.

Unfortunately, this kitchen also had elves living in it. They were too tiny to see, of course, but if you upset them they could be very mischievous indeed. As the broom worked away, it swept into one dark corner where the elves were having a party. Suddenly the king elf was swept away from their little table and into the dustpan! The next thing he knew he was being thrown, with all the other rubbish, on to the rubbish tip.

Coughing and spluttering with rage, the king elf finally climbed out from under all the rubbish in the rubbish tip and stood on top of it. He picked the dirt and dust out of his ears and nose, pulled a fish bone from out of his trousers and tried to look as king-like as he could, having just been thrown on to a rubbish tip. "Who did this?" he squeaked at the top of his voice. "I'll make someone very, very sorry indeed," he vowed.

Eventually he made his way back to the house, and into the kitchen again. The other elves looked at the king elf and did their best not to laugh. For the king elf was still looking very dirty and untidy, and still had bits of rubbish stuck all over him. But the other elves knew better than to laugh at the king, because he was likely to cast a bad spell on them if they did.

"It was the broom that did it," chorused all the other elves.

"Right," said the king elf, "then I'm going to cast a bad spell on the broom."

The broom was by now back in its cupboard. The king elf marched over to the cupboard and jumped in through the keyhole. The king elf pointed to the broom and said,

"Bubble, bubble, gubble, gubble,

Go and cause a lot of trouble!"

And with that the broom suddenly stood to attention, its bristles quivering. It was night time now and everyone in the house was asleep. The broom opened its cupboard door and sprang into the kitchen. It then unlocked the kitchen door and went outside. Straight to the rubbish tip it went, and with a flick of its bristles, swept a huge pile of rubbish back into the kitchen. Tin cans, dirt, dust, chicken bones and goodness knows what else all got swept on to the kitchen floor. The broom then closed the kitchen door, took itself back to its cupboard and all was quiet until morning.

When the maid came down into the kitchen, she couldn't believe her eyes. "Who has made this awful mess?" she said. "If I find out it was those cats . . ." she threatened. She took the broom from the cupboard and swept all the rubbish back outside again.

The next night, the same thing happened. Once it was quiet and everyone in the house was asleep, out of its cupboard came the broom, and into the house came all the rubbish again, swept there as before by the naughty broom. This time, there were fish heads, old bottles and all the soot from the fireplaces.

Well, the maid was speechless. After clearing up again, she got the gardener to burn all the rubbish from the rubbish tip, so that nothing else could be brought in – although she still had no idea how it had happened.

That very night, the naughty broom decided it would make a mess in a different way. So instead of sweeping in rubbish from outside, the broom flew up to the shelves and knocked all the jars to the ground. With a crash they fell to the floor, one after another, and spread their contents everywhere.

"Stop this AT ONCE!" demanded a voice suddenly.

The broom stopped its mischief.

"What do you think you are doing?" said the voice again. The voice had come from a very stern-looking fairy who was now standing on the draining board, with her hands on her hips. What the broom did not know was that one of the bottles it had knocked down contained a good fairy, imprisoned by the elves. Now she was at last free, the spell was broken and it was her turn to cast a spell.

76

"Broom, broom, sweep this floor,
Make it cleaner than ever before.
Find the elves that cast your spell,
And sweep them off into the well," she chanted.

The broom went to work. It seemed to sweep so fast that its bristles just became a blur. Into this corner it went, then into that, and into every nook and cranny it swept. Every bit of dirt and dust, and all the broken bottles, were swept into the dustpan and then out of the house. Then it came back and swept all the elves down into the well where they couldn't do any more mischief.

In the morning, the maid came down to find a spotlessly clean kitchen. She was puzzled to find some of the jars missing, but between you and me she was also rather pleased. It just meant that there were fewer things to dust.

Buried Treasure

Jim lived in a big old house with a big rambling garden. The house was rather spooky, and Jim much preferred the garden. He would spend hours kicking a football around the overgrown lawn, climbing the old apple trees in the orchard or just staring into the pond in case he might spot a fish. It was a wonderful garden to play in but Jim was not really a happy child because he was lonely. How he wished he had someone to play with! It would be such fun to play football with a friend, or have someone to go fishing with. He had plenty of friends at school, but it was a long bus journey to his home and besides, his school friends found his house so spooky that they only came to visit once.

One day Jim was hunting about in the garden with a stick. He hoped he might find some interesting small creatures to examine. Every time he found a new creature he would draw it and try to find out its name. So far, he had discovered eight types of snails and six different ladybirds. As he was poking about under some leaves he saw a piece of metal sticking out of the ground. He reached down and pulled it free. In his hand lay a rusty old key. It was quite big, and as Jim brushed away the soil, he saw that it was carved with beautiful patterns.

Jim carried the key indoors and cleaned it and polished it. Then he set about trying to find the lock that it fitted. First he tried the old garden gate that had been locked as long as Jim could remember. But the key was far too small. Next he tried the grandfather clock in the hall. But the key did not fit the clock's lock. Then he remembered an old wind-up teddy bear that played the drum. Jim hadn't played with the toy for a long time and he eagerly tried out the key, but this time it was too big.

Then Jim had another idea. "Perhaps the key fits something in the attic," he thought. He was usually too scared to go into the attic on his own because it really was scary. But now he was so determined to find the key's home that he ran up the stairs boldly and opened the door. The attic was dimly lit, dusty and full of cobwebs. The water pipes hissed and creaked and Jim shivered. He began to look under a few dustsheets and opened some old boxes, but didn't find anything that looked like it needed a key to unlock it. Then he caught sight of a large book sticking out from one of the shelves. It was one of those sorts of books fitted with a lock. Jim lifted down the book, which was extremely heavy, and put it on the floor. His fingers trembled as he put the key in the lock. It fitted perfectly. He turned the key and the lock sprang open, releasing a cloud of dust. Jim wiped the dust from his eyes, slowly opened the book and turned the pages.

What a disappointment! The pages were crammed with tiny writing and there were no pictures at all. Jim was about to shut the book again when he heard a voice. The voice was coming from the book! "You have unlocked my secrets," it said. "Step into my pages if you are looking for adventure."

Jim was so curious that he found himself stepping on to the book. As soon as he put his foot on the pages he found himself falling through the book. The next thing he knew he was on the deck of a ship. He looked up and saw a tattered black flag flying from a flagpole and on the flag were a skull and crossbones. He was on a pirate ship! He looked down and saw that he was dressed like a pirate.

The pirate ship was sailing along nicely, when suddenly Jim saw some dangerous-looking rocks in the water – and they were heading straight for them! Before he could shout, the ship had run aground and all the pirates were jumping overboard and swimming to the shore. Jim swam, too.

The water felt deliciously warm and when he reached the shore he found warm sand between his toes. He couldn't believe it! Here he was on a desert island. The pirates went in all directions, searching for something to make a shelter. Jim looked, too, and under a rock he found a book. The book looked familiar to Jim. He was sure he'd seen it somewhere before. He was still puzzling over it when one of the pirates came running towards him waving a knife. "You thief, you stole me rubies!" cursed the pirate in a menacing voice. What was Jim to do?

Then he heard a voice call out from the book, "Quick! Step into my pages." Without thinking twice, Jim stepped into the book and suddenly he was back in the attic again.

Jim peered closely at the page from which he'd just stepped. *The Pirates and the Stolen Treasure* it said at the top of the page. Jim read the page and found he was reading exactly the adventure he had been in. He turned excitedly to the contents page at the front of the book and read the chapter titles. *Journey to Mars*, he read, and *The Castle Under the Sea*. Further down it said: *The Magic Car* and *Into the Jungle*. Jim was thrilled. He realised that he could open the book at any page and become part of the adventure, and he only had to find the book and step into it to get back to the attic again.

After that, Jim had many, many adventures. He made lots of friends in the stories and he had lots of narrow escapes. But he always found the book again just in time. Jim was never lonely again.

The Very Big Parcel

Once upon a time there lived an old man and his wife. They dwelled in a small house with a small, neat garden and they were very contented. What's more, they had very good friends and neighbours, with whom they shared everything. One day, there was a knock at the door and there stood the postman with a huge parcel in his arms.

"My, oh my!" exclaimed the old man to his wife as he staggered into the kitchen with the enormous load.

"Whatever can it be?" wondered the old woman as the two of them stared at the parcel. "Perhaps it's a new set of china," said she.

"Or a new wheelbarrow," said he. And they began to think about all the fancy things there might be inside the parcel.

"Well, why don't we open it and see?" said the old lady at last. And so they did. They looked into the box and at first it seemed to be totally empty.

"Well, I never did!" cried the old man. And then he spotted something right in the corner of the box. He lifted it out into the light to examine it more carefully and discovered it was a single seed.

Well, the old man and his wife were most upset. Whereas before they were quite content, now that they had thought about all the things that might have been in the box they were bitterly disappointed by the seed. "Still," said the old man at last, "we'd better plant it anyway. Who knows, maybe we'll get a nice fresh lettuce from it."

So he planted the seed in the garden. Every day he watered the ground and soon a shoot appeared. The shoot grew into a strong young plant and then it grew taller and taller. Higher and higher it grew until it was a handsome tree. The man and his wife were excited to see fruits growing on the tree. "I wonder if they're apples," the old man said. Each day he watered the tree and examined the fruits. One day he said to his wife, "The first fruit is ready to pick." He carefully reached up into the tree and picked the large red fruit.

He carried it into the kitchen and put it on the table. Then he took a knife and cut the fruit in half. To his astonishment out poured a pile of gold coins. "Come quickly!" he called to his wife. Well, the pair of them danced round the kitchen for joy.

The old couple decided to spend just one gold coin and keep the rest. "After all," said the woman wisely, "we don't know what's in the other fruits. They may be full of worms." So they spent one golden penny in the town and put the rest aside.

The next day the old man picked another big red fruit and this, too, was full of gold. After that the old couple were less careful with their money, thinking all the fruits must be full of gold.

They had a wonderful time buying fine clothes and things for the house and garden. Each day the man picked another fruit. Each day it was full of gold and each day they went into town and had a grand time spending the money. But all the while the man forgot entirely to water the tree.

Meanwhile, the old couple's friends and neighbours started to gossip among themselves. They wondered where all the money was coming from and they began to resent the old couple. They noticed that the old couple didn't buy anything for their friends, or even throw a party. Gradually their friends ignored them until the old couple were left with no friends at all. But they didn't even notice because they were so busy spending the gold coins.

Then one day the old man looked out into the garden and saw that the tree was all withered. He rushed outside and threw bucket after bucket of water over the tree, but all to no avail.

87

He and his wife frantically picked the fruits left on the tree, but when they took them indoors they found to their dismay that they were cracked and gnarled. When they broke open the fruits they were full of dust. "If only I had not been so thoughtless and remembered to water the tree!" cried the old man in anguish.

The next day the old couple looked out of the window to find that the tree had vanished. Now what were they to do? They had completely neglected to take care of their garden and now they had nothing to eat. They realised that they would have to sell their riches to buy food. Then they also needed new gardening tools, for theirs had grown rusty with neglect.

As the weeks passed, the old man and his wife gradually sold all the fine things they had bought, just to keep body and soul together. They felt truly miserable and sorry for the way they had treated their neighbours. For now they realised just how lonely they were without their friends. "We have no money now," said the wife one day, "but let's have a party anyway. For friendship is more valuable than any amount of gold coins."

So the old couple invited all their friends and neighbours round and they had a grand party. The friends wondered what had happened to all the old couple's riches and what had happened to make the old couple so friendly once more, but I don't think they ever found out, do you?

The Castle in the Clouds

There was once a family that lived in a little house in a village at the bottom of a mountain. At the top of the mountain was a great, grey castle made of granite. The castle was always shrouded in clouds, so it was known as the castle in the clouds. From the village you could only just see the outline of its high walls and turrets. No-one in the village ever went near the castle, for it looked such a gloomy and forbidding place.

Now in this family there were seven children. One by one they went out into the world to seek their fortune, and at last it was the youngest child's turn. His name was Sam. His only possession was a pet cat named Jess, and she was an excellent rat-catcher. Sam was most upset at the thought of leaving Jess behind when he went off to find work, but then he had an idea.

"I'll offer Jess's services at the castle in the clouds. They're bound to need a good ratter, and I'm sure I can find work there, too," he thought.

His parents were dismayed to discover that Sam intended to seek work at the castle, but try as they might they could not change his mind. So Sam set off for the castle with Jess at his side. Soon the road started to wind up the mountainside through thick pine forests. It grew cold and misty. Rounding a bend they suddenly found themselves up against a massive, grey stone wall. They followed the curve of the wall until they came to the castle door.

Sam went up to the door and banged on it. The sound echoed spookily. "Who goes there?" said a voice.

Looking up, Sam saw that a window high in the wall had been thrown open and a face was eyeing him suspiciously.

"I… I… I wondered if you'd be interested in employing my cat as a rat-catcher," began Sam.

The window slammed shut, but a moment later a hand beckoned him through the partly open castle door. Stepping inside, Sam and Jess found themselves face-to-face with an old man. "Rat-catcher, did you say?" said the old man raising one eyebrow. "Very well, but she'd better do a good job or my master will punish us all!"

Sam sent Jess off to prove her worth. In the meantime Sam asked the old man, who was the castle guard, if there might be any work for him, too.

"You can help out in the kitchens. It's hard work, mind!" the guard said.

Sam was soon at work in the kitchens – and what hard work it was! He spent all day peeling vegetables, cleaning pans and scrubbing the floor. By midnight he was exhausted. He was about to find a patch of straw to make his bed, when he noticed Jess wasn't around. He set off in search of her. Down dark passages he went, up winding staircases, looking in every corner and behind every door, but there was no sign of her. By now he was hopelessly lost and was wondering how he would ever find his way back to the kitchens, when he caught sight of Jess's green eyes shining like lanterns at the top of a rickety spiral staircase. "Here, Jess!" called Sam softly. But Jess stayed just where she was.

When he reached her, he found that she was sitting outside a door and seemed to be listening to something on the other side. Sam put his ear to the door. He could hear the sound of sobbing. He knocked gently at the door. "Who is it?" said a girl's voice.

"I'm Sam, the kitchen boy. What's the matter? Can I come in?" said Sam.

"If only you could," sobbed the voice. "I'm Princess Rose. When my father died my uncle locked me in here so that he could steal the castle. Now I fear I shall never escape!"

Sam pushed and pushed at the door, but to no avail. "Don't worry," he said, "I'll get you out of here."

Sam knew exactly what to do, for when he had been talking to the guard, he had spotted a pair of keys hanging on a nail in the rafters high above the old man's head. He had wondered at the time why anyone should put keys out of the reach of any human hand. Now he thought he knew – but first he had to get the keys himself!

Sam and Jess finally made their way back to where the keys were, only to find the guard was fast asleep in his chair right underneath them! Quick as a flash, Jess had leaped up on to the shelf behind his head. From there, she climbed higher and higher until she reached the rafters. She took the keys in her jaws and carried them gingerly down. But as she jumped from the shelf again, she knocked over a jug and sent it crashing to the floor. The guard woke with a start. "Who goes there?" he growled. He just caught sight of the tip of Jess's tail as she made a dash for the door.

Sam and Jess retraced their steps with the guard in hot pursuit. "You go a different way," hissed Sam, running up the stairs to Rose's door, while the old man disappeared off after Jess. Sam put one of the keys in the lock. It fitted! He turned the key and opened the door. There stood the loveliest girl he had ever seen. The princess ran towards him, as he cried, "Quick!

There's not a moment to lose." He grabbed her hand
and led her out of the tower.

"Give me the keys," she said. She led him down to the
castle cellars. At last they came to a tiny door. The
princess put the second key in the lock and the
door opened. Inside was a small cupboard, and
inside that was a golden casket filled with precious
jewels. "My own casket – stolen by my uncle," cried Rose.

Grabbing the casket the pair ran to the stables and saddled a
horse. Suddenly Jess appeared with the guard still chasing him.
With a mighty leap Jess landed on the back of the horse behind
the princess and Sam. "Off we go!" cried Sam.

And that was the last that any of them saw of the castle in
the clouds. Sam married the princess and they all lived happily
ever after.